King Midas

Julia Jarman and Claudia Venturini

W
FRANKLIN WATTS
LONDON•SYDNEY

Chapter 1:
A Foolish King

Long, long ago in a land called Phrygia,
there lived a king called Midas. He was
rich and kind – but sometimes very foolish.
He often spoke without thinking first, so he
said silly things.

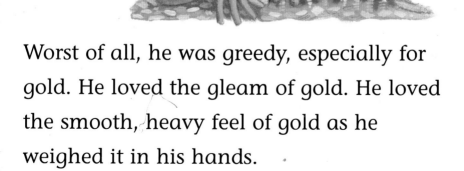

Worst of all, he was greedy, especially for
gold. He loved the gleam of gold. He loved
the smooth, heavy feel of gold as he
weighed it in his hands.

King Midas lived in a splendid palace with his daughter, Zoe. He loved Zoe even more than he loved his rose garden, which was famous throughout the land. He loved her even more than his gold. Of course he did, and Zoe loved her father.

Every morning they walked in the garden together, admiring the perfumed roses. They stroked their velvety petals and breathed in their delicious perfumes. Sometimes Midas would pick a rose and give it to Zoe.

"It is lovely but you are lovelier," he would say to her.

Chapter 2:
A Strange Visitor

One morning when they were walking, they found a strange creature sleeping in the rose garden. He had horns and hairy legs, and he was snoring loudly.

"What is that?" Zoe asked, and her
father smiled.
"It is the old satyr, Silenus."
He explained that a satyr was
half man and half goat.

"I have a terrible headache!" Silenus
whimpered as he woke up.
"You drank too much wine last night,
Silenus," laughed the king.

As they helped him to his feet, Midas told Zoe that Silenus was a friend of Dionysus, the god of wine. That is why he drank so much of it. And suddenly …

… there was a flash of lightning and a strange being descended on a billowing cloud strewn with grapes. More grapes adorned his head and he sipped from a sparkling glass of wine.

King Midas dropped to his knees.
"Daughter, it's the god himself. It is
Dionysus. He has come from the home of
the gods, Mount Olympus, to visit us.
Kneel daughter, kneel and thank the god for
honouring us with his presence."

But the god boomed, "No, Midas. It is for me to thank you for looking after my old friend, Silenus."

Dionysus had a voice like thunder.

"Make a wish for anything you like," he boomed again. "And I will grant it! That is my reward to you for your kindness."

"Anything?" said Midas, who couldn't
believe his luck. "Anything at all?"
"Yes, anything," repeated the god.

Chapter 3:
King Midas's Wish

"Then I wish for everything I touch to turn to gold," said Midas quickly.

"Are you sure?" boomed Dionysus. "I can give you time to think about it."

But King Midas didn't want to think. He just wanted to be the richest person in the world. He wanted to have more lustrous gold than anyone else in the world.

With a frown the god granted his wish.
He pointed his finger at Midas and – FLASH!
– he gave the king the golden touch.
And from that moment on, King Midas's
troubles began.

At first he was delighted.

He touched a table and it turned to gold.

He touched a couch and it turned to gold.
He walked around his palace and
everything he touched became gold.
"Wonderful!" he cried. "I'll soon be the
richest man in Phrygia!"

Chapter 4:
The Golden Touch

Soon after that King Midas wandered into his garden and touched one of his lovely red roses. It turned to gold.
He touched a pink rose and it turned to gold.

He touched a white rose and it turned to gold. He did not notice that he could no longer smell the roses' delicious scent.

He did not notice that he could no longer feel their soft velvety petals.

"I am the richest man in Greece!" he cried, when all his rose bushes were solid gold. "But I want to be even richer!"

He put his hand in the fountain, and the water turned to gold.

By now he was feeling hungry. Joyfully
he went into dinner and picked up a juicy
chicken leg.

Crunch – his teeth jarred against
something hard.

Even now he did not stop to think.
He felt thirsty so he lifted a goblet of wine to
his lips – and felt hard metal in his mouth.

Only now did King Midas start to worry.

Zoe was worried too.

"Father, what have you done?" she cried,
rushing to his side.

She put her arms around him and …

… she turned to gold. Only then, with his beloved daughter hard and cold and stiff and lifeless in his arms, did Midas realise how foolish and greedy he had been.

"I'm sorry," he cried. "I'm so sorry!"

But Zoe could not hear him.

Chapter 5:
King Midas's Sadness

Now shame and sadness filled the king's sorry heart.

"Dionysus! Dionysus! Come and help me!" He begged the god to come down from the clouds on Mount Olympus.

"Undo the stupid wish I made!"

It was a while before the god appeared,
for gods do not like undoing wishes.
"I warned you to think before you spoke,"
he said.
"I know and I have learned my lesson,"
said Midas.
"Mmmm," said the god. "You could try
going down to the river and covering
yourself with water."

King Midas thought about it. He thought hard. He really had learned the lesson. What if the water in the river turned to gold? What if all the water in the kingdom turned to gold?

What if he turned to gold?

But then he thought about Zoe.
Life without her was too painful. He must
take the risk. So he rushed to the river,
hugging her golden body. He plunged into
the water and …

... the water didn't turn to gold.
Nor did the river bank. Nor did he.

Best of all, his beloved daughter came
back to life.
"Father!" she sighed as her lovely, soft
lips framed the words. "Thank you."

King Midas's golden touch had gone!

But even now some people do say that
the water in that faraway river has a
golden gleam.

About the story

The figure of ancient King Midas is surrounded by many legends. It is thought that he lived in the 8th century BCE. This story of *King Midas* is a Greek myth, which is told by the Roman poet Ovid in his book *Metamorphoses.* In this long poem, Ovid tries to tell the history of the world from the very beginning to the death of Julius Caesar in the first century CE. There are more than 250 myths in Ovid's book. Another myth about Midas tells of the time after he has lost his golden touch. He now hates riches and lives in the countryside. He loves music but gets into an argument about it and the god Apollo gives him donkey's ears!

Be in the story!

Imagine you are
Zoe. What might you
be thinking when your
father makes his
foolish wish?

Now imagine you are Zoe
when you have just been
turned back from being
a golden statue.
Write a letter
about your
week, beginning
with a quiet walk in
the rose garden!

First published in 2014 by
Franklin Watts
338 Euston Road
London
NW1 3BH

Franklin Watts Australia
Level 17/207 Kent Street
Sydney
NSW 2000

A CIP catalogue record for this book is available
from the British Library.

The artwork for this story first appeared in
Hopscotch Myths: King Midas' Golden Touch

ISBN 978 1 4451 3005 7 (hbk)
ISBN 978 1 4451 3008 8 (pbk)
ISBN 978 1 4451 3007 1 (library ebook)
ISBN 978 1 4451 3006 4 (ebook)

Series Editor: Jackie Hamley
Series Advisor: Catherine Glavina
Series Designer: Cathryn Gilbert

Printed in China

Franklin Watts is a divison of
Hachette Children's Books,
an Hachette UK company.
www.hachette.co.uk